CW00855019

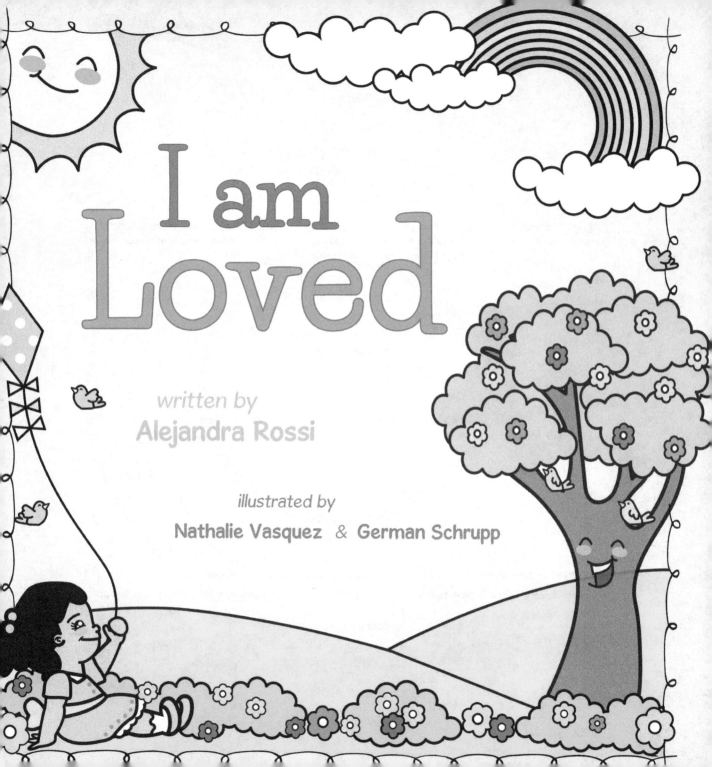

I am Loved

written by
Alejandra Rossi

illustrated by
Nathalie Vasquez & **German Schrupp**

I am Loved—Copyright ©2021 by Alejandra Rossi
Published by UNITED HOUSE Publishing

All rights reserved. No portion of this book may be reproduced or shared in any form—electronic, printed, photocopied, recording, or by any information storage and retrieval system, without prior written permission from the publisher. The use of short quotations is permitted.

ISBN: 978-1-952840-05-0

UNITED HOUSE Publishing
Waterford, Michigan
info@unitedhousepublishing.com
www.unitedhousepublishing.com

Cover and interior illustrations: Nathalie Vasquez and German Schrupp
Cover and interior formatting: Matt Russell, Marketing Image, mrussell@marketing-image.com

Published in Waterford, MI
Printed in the United States

2021—First Edition

SPECIAL SALES
Most UNITED HOUSE books are available at special quantity discounts when purchased in bulk by corporations, organizations, and special-interest groups. For information, please e-mail orders@unitedhousepublishing.com

Dedicated to the One who loved us first,
With an unconditional, everlasting love.

THIS BOOK BELONGS TO :

_____

You ask the sun to shine for me
and the clouds to go away.
You tell birds to serenade me
With sweet songs along the way.

I am loved by You.

You made the water clear
Like a mirror on the wall
I see how beautiful You made me,
I will now stand proud and tall.

I am loved by You.

You made the mountains high,
And give me the strength to climb.
I know You're looking down at me,
While painting rainbows in the sky.

I am loved by You.

You tell the stars to light up the dark,
I count them one by one
You ask the moon to watch over me,
While I dream about the sun.

I am loved by You.

You made the oceans deep,
Vast and endless like your love,
The waves can never get me down
For I am standing on the rock.
I am loved by You.

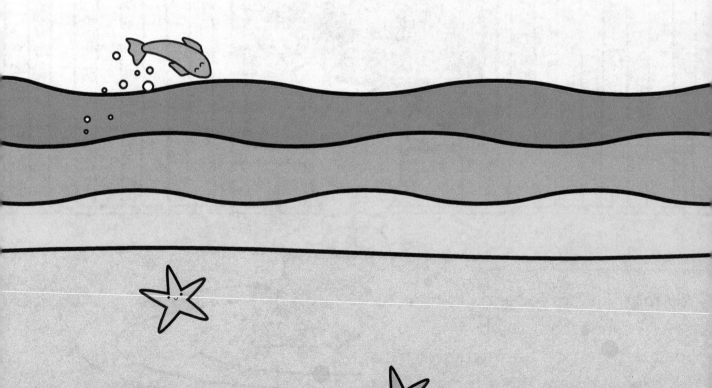

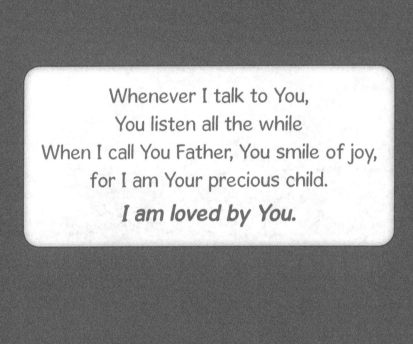

Whenever I talk to You,
You listen all the while
When I call You Father, You smile of joy,
for I am Your precious child.

I am loved by You.

When I read a Word about You,
I learn about Your love for me.
You gave Your life away,
To save us and set us free.

I am loved by You.

Wherever I go, no matter the distance,
You walk beside me there.
When I walk through the darkness,
You are the light that guides with care.

I am loved by You.

When I feel lost,
You guide me home.
When I feel weak,
You give me hope.
I am loved by You.

You made the cloudy days,
For me to appreciate the sun
I can see your blessings in my life
Like rain pouring from above.

I am loved by You.

When I go through storms,
You are my shelter, my rest.
I am never alone,
You protect the best.
I am loved by You.

Finish

When I fall, You pick me up,
You help me to stand strong.
When I cry, You wipe my tears,
You were here all along.

I am loved by You.

You love me just the way I am,
However I look, say, or do.
Everywhere I go, I find Your love,
Father, I am loved by You.

the
Author

Alejandra Rossi is a passionate Christian writer and designer who holds a Master's in Architecture from Virginia Tech. Since she was young, she has had a passion for writing and books, a seed that was planted by her grandparents. She loves nature, art, running, and being a tourist in her own city. She currently lives in Fairfax, Virginia with her family where she works at an architecture firm and attends Cathedral of Faith Ministries.

She is the author of I am Loved, a children's book that inspires young readers to discover and learn about God and His love for all of us, a message she believes will strengthen the identity and self-image of the next generation. To learn more about her, visit her blog mylovewell.com or follow her on Instagram @rossi_alee.

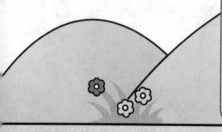

Nathalie Vasquez and German Schrupp are Bolivian designers and illustrators who reside in Santa Cruz, Bolivia. They are the founders and owners of Totus Tuus Maria, a designer gift shop focused on religious products designed and illustrated by them. They are inspired by regional and international religious images, giving them their own emotive and cute style. Follow them online @totustusmaria_scz on Instagram.

CPSIA information can be obtained
at www.ICGtesting.com
Printed in the USA
LVHW061736080421
683893LV00004B/357

9 781952 840050